AMERICAN VALUES AND FREEDOMS

THE RIGHT TO
PROTEST

by DUCHESS HARRIS, JD, PHD

Essential Library

An Imprint of Abdo Publishing | abdopublishing.com

ABDOPUBLISHING.COM

Published by Abdo Publishing, a division of ABDO, PO Box 398166, Minneapolis, Minnesota 55439. Copyright © 2018 by Abdo Consulting Group, Inc. International copyrights reserved in all countries. No part of this book may be reproduced in any form without written permission from the publisher. Essential Library™ is a trademark and logo of Abdo Publishing.

Printed in the United States of America, North Mankato, Minnesota
102017
012018

Interior Photos: Bettmann/Getty Images, 4–5, 39; Popperfoto/Getty Images, 6; AP Images, 8, 11, 56, 62; Everett Collection/Newscom, 14, 64, 69; Leif Skoogfors/Corbis Historical/Getty Images, 17; iStockphoto, 18, 35; Diego G. Diaz/Shutterstock Images, 19; North Wind Picture Archives, 20–21; Everett Historical/Shutterstock Images, 23, 41, 49; Mannie Garcia/AFP/Getty Images, 24; Federal Works Agency/Work Projects Administration/Division of Information/National Archives and Record Administration, 29; Pamela Au/Shutterstock Images, 32–33; Interim Archives/Archives Photos/Getty Images, 37; Stapleton Historical Collection Heritage Images/Newscom, 46–47; American Photo Archive/Alamy, 52; Ms. Jane Campbell/Shutterstock Images, 54; Gene Herrick/AP Images, 60; UPI Glasshouse Images/Newscom, 66–67; AFP/Getty Images, 73; Ramin Talaie/Corbis Historical/Getty Images, 76–77; Lucas Jackson/Reuters/Newscom, 78; David Goldman/AP Images, 82–83; Shutterstock Images, 84; Stephen Maturen/Getty Images News/Getty Images, 88–89; Morry Gash/AP Images, 93; Lynne Sladky/AP Images, 95; Erik Mcgregor/Pacific Press/Newscom, 96

Editor: Claire Mathiowetz
Series Designer: Becky Daum
Contributor: Wil Mara

Publisher's Cataloging-in-Publication Data

Names: Harris, Duchess, author.
Title: The right to protest / by Duchess Harris.
Description: Minneapolis, Minnesota : Abdo Publishing, 2018. | Series: American values and freedoms | Online resources and index.
Identifiers: LCCN 2017946728 | ISBN 9781532113031 (lib.bdg.) | ISBN 9781532151910 (ebook)
Subjects: LCSH: Demonstrations–Law and legislation–Juvenile literature. | Protest movements–United States–Juvenile literature. | Civil rights–Juvenile literature. | Constitutional law–United States–Juvenile literature.
Classification: DDC 303.484–dc23
LC record available at https://lccn.loc.gov/2017946728

CONTENTS

CHAPTER 1

GUNNED DOWN

Students and faculty run for cover as National Guard forces throw tear gas at Kent State University on May 4, 1970.

By noon on May 4, 1970, the rage at Kent State University in Ohio was reaching an alarming level. An hour earlier, more than 200 students had gathered on the Commons, a large area of open land between several campus buildings. Now there were approximately 3,000 people either actively demonstrating or supporting those who were.[1]

They came to peacefully protest, as was their right guaranteed by the First Amendment of the US Constitution. They were angered by the United States' ongoing involvement in the war in Vietnam. The current president, Richard Nixon, had promised during the election of 1968 to end the war. But on April 30, he announced that instead he was going to expand the war by sending US troops into the nation of Cambodia. This angered millions of students around the country because so many young people had already been drafted by the government to take part in the war and had died.

The Kent State students were also angered by the continuing presence of the Ohio National Guard at their college. Days before, the guard had been sent to keep them

Some students retaliated by picking up the tear gas canisters and throwing them back at the guardsmen.

and other protesters around the town of Kent under control. The guardsmen used force to do so, including tear gas and nightsticks. Some protesters fought back, and a few were injured. Now, tempers were rapidly rising on both sides.

THE OPENING CONFRONTATION

A military jeep pulled up to the crowd and the students were ordered to go back to their classes and their dorms. Very few obeyed, however, believing they were well within their rights to continue protesting. They yelled back at the guardsmen but refused to move. A few students threw rocks.

The man in command of the National Guard that day, General Robert Canterbury, gave the order to disperse the protesters. The guardsmen attempted to do this first by throwing canisters of tear gas. Tear gas is a chemical weapon that causes severe stinging and tearing in the eyes. Under direct or prolonged exposure, it can also cause blindness, respiratory and skin irritations, and even some bleeding. It is commonly used in riot control because its effects are unpleasant but, the great majority of the time, temporary. (Tear gas continues to be used by US police in riot situations today, despite the fact that it was banned from international use in 1997 by the Chemical Weapons Convention. The primary reason for its continual use, experts say, is because a more

The mayor of Kent declared the town in a state of emergency due to the protesters' actions.

effective agent has not yet been developed.) But the wind blew most of the tear gas away from the protesters. The attempted use of the gas served to further encourage them, and the protesters began throwing another round of rocks. A few students even picked up the smoking gas canisters and threw them back at the guardsmen. This, however, also had little effect, as the guardsmen were equipped with gas masks.

In response to the protesters' refusal to disperse, approximately 75 of the roughly 100 guardsmen present began moving toward the protesters with their rifles aimed, the bayonets extended.[2] Frightened by this aggression, the protesters ran up and over a nearby hill. Once on the other side, they turned left and headed for the open areas in front of two campus buildings. The guardsmen continued to pursue them over the hill. This eventually brought them to a practice field that was used for various sports. Most importantly, however, it was surrounded by a chain-link fence—which meant the guardsmen now had no place to go.

IT ALL GOES WRONG

Approximately ten minutes passed. Some of the protesters did as they were told and returned to their classes or dorms. Many others, however, did not. A number remained scattered in front of the two buildings, either on the grassy areas or around the parking lots. But there were also groups who were still angry at the guardsmen and wanted to make sure they knew it. They moved closer to the troops. More rocks and tear gas canisters were thrown.

The troops seemed unsure of what to do at this point. A few of them got down on one knee and raised their rifles in a firing position. They did not fire any shots, but their gestures likely further infuriated the protesters, who felt their lives were being threatened.

The guardsmen finally decided to go back up the hill and return to the Commons area. As they did so, a group of protesters approached them. A few members of the National Guard stopped and watched these students to make sure they didn't come too close. But both sides were angrier than ever, and this is when tragedy occurred.

At 12:24 p.m., one of the guardsmen removed his pistol and began firing at the protesters. Some of the other guardsmen took this to mean the order to fire had been given and began firing their own weapons. Some dropped to their knees in the same combat stance that had been used on the practice field. Terrified students ran in every direction, seeking cover.

The shooting went on for roughly 13 seconds, during which time approximately 67 rounds were fired. When it was over, four students had received fatal wounds. Incredibly, none of the students who had been struck were any closer than 75 feet (23 m) from the guardsmen—nowhere near close enough to be considered a threat.[3]

Students surrounded an injured man after shots rang out.

NOT BLANKS

Many of the students who took part in the protest were under the impression that the weapons carried by the National Guard forces contained blanks. They thought there was no way the guardsmen would use real ammunition on defenseless students. But they soon realized that live bullets were flying everywhere. One student who witnessed the event was later quoted as saying, "[Then] the firing stopped. I lay there maybe 10 or 15 seconds. I got up, I saw four or five students lying around the lot. By this time, it was like mass hysteria. Students were crying, they were screaming for ambulances. I heard some girl screaming, 'They didn't have blanks! They didn't have blanks!' No, they didn't."[4]

After the shooting, students began screaming and crying for help, many pleading for ambulances. And it almost didn't end there—in the wake of the violence, many of the students gathered to launch an all-out attack on the guardsmen, intent on making them pay for their actions. By this time, however, numerous faculty members had arrived on the scene. One in particular, geology professor Glenn Frank, stood between what was then essentially two angry mobs and begged both sides to back down. Had he not done so, it is likely the bloodshed would have continued and the body count would have risen.

IN THE AFTERMATH

The immediate reaction to the Kent State shootings (which soon became known as the Kent State Massacre) around the nation was swift and dramatic. Strikes were held on more than 450 college campuses involving more than four million students.[5] However, many of these strikes—themselves a form of protest— resulted in further injuries. Many of these colleges were forced to close for a time. Kent State was shut down for approximately a month and a half.

In Washington, DC, tens of thousands of protesters marched in response to the killings. These protests also turned violent,

THE DEAD AND WOUNDED

Two of the students who were killed during the Kent State incident, Jeffrey Miller and Allison Krause, had taken part in the protests. Miller was 20 years old and from New York, and he had transferred to Kent from Michigan State. Krause was 19 years old and an honor student, and she and Miller were friends. She had reportedly said, "Flowers are better than bullets," in conversation the day before she died.[6] The other two fatalities, Sandra Scheuer and William Knox Schroeder, had not been protesting at the time of their deaths. They were merely walking from one class to the next. Schroeder was a member of the military himself, part of the school's Reserve Officers' Training Corps (ROTC) program. Another nine students were shot and wounded, one of whom would remain paralyzed for the rest of his life.

Thousands of people gathered for a memorial service days after the massacre.

resulting in millions of dollars' worth of damage to commercial, government, and private property. President Nixon had to be taken out of the city at one point and sequestered at Camp

David, the president's personal retreat, while military forces protected the White House and other key locations. The protesters' violent actions ended up hurting their cause. At the time, the majority of Americans polled for their response to the Kent State shootings believed that the protesters, rather than the National Guard forces, were to blame.

The government launched an investigation into the incident at Kent State, and people on all sides began lawsuits, both civil and criminal. Despite all this legal activity, none of the guardsmen who took part in the shooting received a criminal conviction. The prevailing opinion was that although their actions were unjustified, they felt their own safety was under enough threat to warrant acts of self-defense.

A QUESTION OF BOUNDARIES

There is little doubt the students of Kent State had every right, as afforded them in the Constitution, to stage a peaceful protest in response to President Nixon's military activities in the Vietnam War. But even to this day, the tragedy that unfolded in the wake of those protests has raised questions that are difficult to answer. For example, while the students had every right to make their disapproval of the president's decision known, did that then give them the right to begin acting in a violent manner? If the National Guard forces were acting under

NO CLAIM OF RESPONSIBILITY

During the trial concerning the Kent State incident, General Robert Canterbury testified that he denied any claims of responsibility for the weapons used by the National Guard forces, the fact that the weapons were loaded, or the methods used by the troops to disperse the students who were on the campus. He also stated that his understanding was that the National Guard's role that day was simply to assist campus police, not to assume control of the site. Canterbury was not indicted for his role in the event.

orders from the Ohio state government to keep the protesters under control, then the protesters didn't have the right to direct their anger at them by throwing rocks and other projectiles. But on the contrary, the guardsmen didn't have the right to approach unarmed students with rifles and pistols loaded with live ammunition. Even if the guardsmen had not fired a shot at all, is it constitutional for military forces to descend upon a crowd of defenseless citizens?

Where are the lines and boundaries on both sides—the protesters and those who keep order? And how can these limitations be ensured and not violated in the future? How can the right and privilege to protest be maintained? More importantly, how can we make sure tragedies like the one at Kent State don't happen again?

Demonstrations that were held all over the country after the Kent State Massacre cried out for one thing: peace.

DISCUSSION STARTERS

- How do you think the protesters would have behaved differently if they'd known the guardsmen's weapons contained live ammunition? How do you think the guardsmen would have behaved differently if their weapons had blanks?

- Do you think the guardsmen should have been arrested? Why or why not?

- How do you think both parties could have handled the situation better?

- Can you think of other more recent events that are similar to what happened at Kent State?

THE HOWS AND WHYS OF PROTESTING

REASONS FOR PROTESTS

- The core element that inspires protesting is a set of circumstances or conditions that are deemed unfair by one or more people, so much so that they feel compelled to take some kind of action against it.

- Many protests could be avoided if the people on one side of an issue heeded the anger of those on the other.

- A very common condition for protest is an opponent viewed as having a position of significant power. This opponent is often some type of authoritative institution, such as a corporation, government, or religious organization.

- Those who protest often start out with a feeling of powerlessness that stems directly from the perceived inability to fix an unfair situation on their own. Thus, the urge to protest often begins as a purely passive-aggressive gesture, with the hope that those on the other side will make the necessary and righteous changes on their own.

- The most fundamental element of protesting is having a clear objective. Protesters must focus on where they wish to go once a resolution is reached.

TYPES OF PROTESTS

- **Vigils.** Groups of people gather to protest a cause without any intention of being outwardly hostile or destructive. Vigils may include prayer, chanting, singing, and so on.

Nighttime vigils often include the lighting of candles.

- **Passive protests.** People apply pressure to opponents by exposing potentially damaging information to the public.

- **Public demonstrations.** These, the most common form of protests, have many varieties, including picket lines, marches, and sit-ins.

- **Boycotts.** Protesters cause financial harm to those on the other side of the issue at hand. Boycotts are used most effectively in business situations in which boycotters no longer purchase the opposition's goods or services.

- **Workers' strikes.** Protesters apply financial pressure to an employer (a business) in the hope that the latter will give in to demands. Workers refuse to work and the company begins losing money almost from the moment the strike begins.

- **Legal means.** The objective of legal protests is to force the opposition to cave to the demands through laws and regulations.

- **Civil disobedience.** Protesters take public action that will likely get them into some kind of legal or civil trouble but rarely involves violent or destructive behavior.

Sit-ins are a form of public demonstrations.

- **Violent protests.** Rioting, for example, occurs when a crowd begins causing harm to those they perceive as the enemy, to any type of property connected with the issue at hand, or in some cases, to property that was in the wrong place at the wrong time.

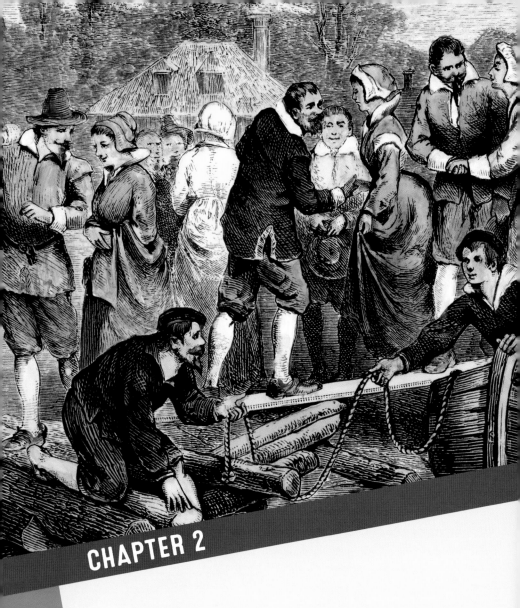

CHAPTER 2

A LONG HISTORY

The Jamestown colony would lay the foundation for the first workers' strike in American history.

America has a long history of protesting. Many people made the decision to come to North America from Europe based on protesting principles. Some were taking action against religious persecution. Rather than convert to the preferred beliefs of their community or their government, they chose to take action and seek a new life in America. There, they could freely worship within the faith of their own choosing. Since colonization began, America has been viewed as a safe haven for political dissenters, victims of discrimination, and those who seek new economic opportunities.

RIGHT FROM THE START

The first permanent settlement occupied by English immigrants in North America was the Jamestown colony. It was founded in May 1607 by English investors, in part because the leadership of England was eager to establish a presence in the New World. The investors were part of the Virginia Company, and they chose approximately 100 English citizens who wanted to build a better life for themselves.[1]

Jamestown is believed to be the site of the very first protest in American history. It was a workers' strike— that is, a refusal of workers to perform their jobs due to dissatisfaction—among the Polish craftsmen of the colony. The Poles had earned a reputation as some of the finest workers around. In fact, John Smith, who played a pivotal role in the founding of Jamestown, was quoted as saying, "There are no better workers than Poles," and he wanted them to be part of Jamestown's development.[2]

Smith had traveled through Poland in 1602 after escaping from imprisonment in Turkey. During his journey, he was deeply impressed by the Poles' skill in trades such as lumber cutting and glassblowing, as well as their tireless work ethic. A few years after Smith helped settle the Jamestown colony, he sent word back to England that he wanted Polish craftsmen included

John Smith had to leave Jamestown in 1609 after suffering an injury.

Because the American Revolution was such a powerful protest, many people get together across the United States to reenact the country's earliest history every year.

in the second group of colonists. No sooner had these Poles arrived than they were constructing houses with wood from the vast pine forests. More Polish workers were recruited, and a robust timber industry rapidly developed. It produced lumber for houses and other construction as well, including some of the colonists' earliest ships.

The early Polish settlers and craftsmen integrated themselves into the Jamestown colony without too much difficulty. Then a problem arose: when the first local elections were held in 1619, the Poles were informed they were not allowed to vote. After all they had given the colony through their sweat and toil, they would have no voice in the choice of their political leadership. The reason, they were told, was because Jamestown was first and foremost a British colony. Thus, only those of British origin could take part in the process. Outraged by this and fully aware of their value to the colony, the Poles undertook the very first formal protest in the New World by refusing to do any further work. The Poles believed they contributed to the colony as much as anyone else and were therefore entitled to be treated as full citizens.

The Virginia General Assembly was alarmed by the Poles' boldness and feared the damage that would be done to the local economy without their participation. The lawmakers quickly got together and reversed the decision, writing, "Upon some dispute of the Polonians resident in Virginia, it is now agreed they shall be enfranchised and made as free as any inhabitant there whatsoever."[3] And thus the first known organized protest in American history ended peacefully with the change desired by the protesters.

A MUCH BIGGER MATTER

The most significant example of protest in early American history is that which led to the American Revolution. This protest led to independence from Britain and the birth of the United States of America.

Starting in 1754, Britain fought a war on North American soil against the military of France. A large number of Native Americans chose to fight alongside the French. This conflict became known as the French and Indian War. At the war's conclusion in 1763, British forces emerged victorious, resulting in the reduction of French influence in the region. In the years that followed, the British government had to address the financial problems related to the war's great cost.

To raise money, they imposed taxes on the British colonists in North America. A well-known example of this was the Stamp Act, issued in 1765. It stated that printed paper products bearing the government's embossed stamp would include an extra fee, also known as a tax. Such products included newspapers, magazines, and playing cards. Since these items could not be easily obtained elsewhere, the colonists had little choice but to pay the tax—at first. They were angry, however, because they had never been burdened with direct taxes before.

The British government eventually withdrew some of these new taxes in response to the colonists'

The colonists' main point of contention in being required to pay taxes to help resolve the financial difficulties of the British government was that they had no representation in Britain. No political representatives in the British government looked after the interests of the colonists. The famous slogan "No taxation without representation" described their feelings about their lack of members in Parliament. The fact that the colonists had also aided the British in the French and Indian War by providing their own soldiers, equipment, and supplies—and all at great cost to themselves—only deepened their resentment.

outrage, but this generosity did not last long. The government determined that it had the right to impose taxes on the colonists without their consent or approval. And it certainly didn't need colonial representatives in British Parliament. So, in 1767, the British government began issuing new taxes. In turn, tension grew between the colonists and the British government. The Townshend Acts of that year put duties on essential products, such as goods made from paper, glass, and lead. These were critical raw materials at that time. The acts also taxed popular food items, such as tea.

Resentment among the colonists intensified, and some now-legendary acts of protest resulted. One of the most consequential is known today as the Boston Massacre. It occurred on March 5, 1770, when an angry crowd surrounded a group of British soldiers. The colonists began throwing rocks and other objects at the soldiers. The soldiers responded by firing their rifles. When the incident was over, three colonists lay dead and another two later died from their wounds.

CRISPUS ATTUCKS

One of the three men killed during the Boston Massacre was Crispus Attucks. Historians believe Attucks was either of full African-American heritage or the offspring of a mixed-race couple. Little is known of Attucks's early life, although there is some evidence that he was a slave who in 1750 escaped his bondage at a farm in Framingham, Massachusetts. He spent some time working on docks along the Atlantic coast, possibly under the assumed name of Michael Johnson. He was in Boston after returning from a trip to the Bahamas when the conflict occurred. Considered the first casualty of the American Revolution, his death and those of the other two colonists served to heighten anti-British sentiment. Attucks was also elevated as a martyr figure during the abolition movements of the mid-1800s.

An engraving depicts Crispus Attucks at the center of the Boston Massacre.

THE BOSTON TEA PARTY

A less violent but equally famous act of protest during this time was the Boston Tea Party. In May 1773, the British government issued the Tea Act. The colonists had little choice but to purchase their tea from the British East India Company. The act gave exclusive shipping rights to the company, making matters difficult for those who relied on other tea sources as part of their income. Tensions reached a breaking point on the night of December 16, 1773. A band of approximately 60 angry colonists—some of whom were costumed as Native Americans—assembled near Boston Harbor.[4] Word had spread that a meeting was being held to address the problems caused by the Tea Act. The colonists consisted of radicals, who were determined to push for independence from Britain, and the more conservative colonial merchants. Encouraged by a large and angry crowd, they went down to Griffin's Wharf and boarded three ships loaded with British East India Company tea. They broke open the crates with hatchets and dumped the contents into the water.

THE INTOLERABLE ACTS

Word of the events of the Boston Tea Party did not reach the British government until January 1774. Its immediate action was one of outrage, resulting in the issuance of the Coercive Acts. Rebellious colonists also called them the Intolerable Acts. The majority of the Intolerable Acts were a direct response to the Boston Tea Party. For example, they declared Boston Harbor closed until the value of the destroyed tea was repaid in full. Another facet of the Intolerable Acts brought the governance of Massachusetts under full control of the British government, requiring that all positions be appointed and approved by British civil servants. This meant that almost no colonists would have been able to occupy any of these positions. In the end, these acts only fueled the already growing hostility colonists harbored toward British leadership.

Despite the number of people involved, only one arrest was made. All other participants successfully fled the scene.

The relationship between the British and the colonists worsened until the colonists declared themselves a free and independent nation. They did this not only through the Declaration of Independence, but also by fielding their own soldiers in order to resist the inevitable British military response to their actions. The conflict, which became known as the American Revolutionary War, ended with a colonial victory in 1783. But unlike the striking of Polish artisans in Jamestown, this protest led to the death of tens of thousands of people on both sides.

DISCUSSION STARTERS

- What could the early colonial government have done at Jamestown to avoid the conflict with the Polish craftsmen? How could these lessons be applied to avoiding protest movements in the United States in the future?

- The British government needed money in the wake of the French and Indian War. Was it justified in taxing the colonists? Was the British government justified in using force against the colonists prior to the outbreak of the war?

- Would you have participated in the Boston Tea Party if asked? Why or why not?

TURMOIL IN THE 1800s

When the colonies broke free from Britain and earned their independence, the spirit of the American people came into fruition. The Founding Fathers had protesting in mind when they wrote the First Amendment in the Bill of Rights. It guaranteed the right of free speech, the right to assemble peaceably, and the right to petition against government policies that are perceived to be unfair.

While the issue of independence had been settled, there were still other issues that needed to be addressed.

Throughout much of the 1800s, one of the most serious problems facing the country was that of slavery.

A TERRIBLE INSTITUTION

The enslavement of African Americans in North America started almost from the beginning of colonization. In 1619, approximately two dozen Africans were forcibly brought to Jamestown by a Dutch ship and sold to the colonists.[1] Throughout the rest of the 1600s and into the 1700s, the slave trade swelled and flourished. Slavery was particularly prevalent in the South, where agriculture was the heartbeat of the economy and slaves provided the necessary labor at relatively little cost. However, there was slavery throughout the country. Slaves were subjected to horrifying working and living conditions, and many were openly mistreated at the hands of their owners. Slaves weren't recognized as citizens, and thus they were denied many of the rights and privileges of other Americans.

Throughout this time, some people felt slavery was inherently immoral. By the mid to late 1700s, many such people had worked their way into positions of influence and tried to push an abolitionist agenda. Despite the fact that slavery had been legal in all 13 colonies at the start of the Revolutionary War, thousands of African Americans fought

ONA JUDGE

One of the most inspiring figures during America's slavery era was Oney "Ona" Judge. She was born on George Washington's Virginia plantation, Mount Vernon, sometime in the early 1770s. Her mother was an African-American slave and her father a white indentured servant, and both worked for Washington at the time of Judge's birth. Affable and intelligent, Judge eventually became the personal servant to Martha Washington, George's wife. When she was 16, she and six other Mount Vernon slaves were taken to New York after George became America's first president. A short time later, when the nation's capital was relocated to Philadelphia, Judge moved again with the Washingtons. While Judge was not treated as badly as some slaves were, her greatest wish was to be free. In 1796, however, after learning that she was to be given to Martha Washington's granddaughter as a wedding gift, Judge decided the only way to achieve her freedom was to escape. She did so in the spring, while the Washingtons were getting ready to leave

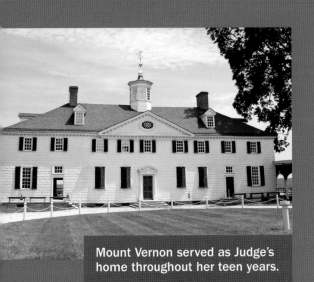

Mount Vernon served as Judge's home throughout her teen years.

Philadelphia and return with all their slaves to Virginia. She was aided by many free African Americans and other sympathetic abolitionists. Although the Washingtons made every effort to find her, Judge was never caught. She eventually made her way to New Hampshire, where she lived the rest of her life as a fugitive—but a free one.

alongside whites against the British. Their hope was that the spirit of independence would lead to their freedom in the war's aftermath. When this didn't happen, the resentment that most enslaved people felt toward their enslavers began to intensify. It didn't help that the very nature of slave life was beginning to change around this time. The invention of the cotton gin, which was patented in 1794, meant cotton output in the South was expected to increase. To meet the growing demand, more slaves were used than ever before (by 1850 there were more than three million).[2]

A BREAKING POINT

Finally, in the North, some abolitionist sentiment worked its way into the law. Vermont took the first bold step, abolishing slavery in 1777. In the early 1780s, Pennsylvania, Massachusetts, New Hampshire, Rhode Island, and Connecticut all enacted legislation that began to do likewise. By the early 1800s, slavery had been rendered illegal in all Northern states. In the South, however, it continued as before—and many slaves, along with those in the South who sympathized with them, were reaching their breaking point.

The first significant protest in the South was an uprising led by Nat Turner in August 1831. Turner had spent his life as a slave on a plantation in Virginia. He was highly intelligent and, as he grew older, deeply religious. He soon became convinced that God had put him on Earth for the divine purpose of leading a rebellion against white slave owners. With a natural gift for persuasion, he assembled a force of approximately 70 other African Americans.[3] On the night of August 21, they went from house to house in Turner's neighborhood, freeing the slaves and killing most of the whites with sharp tools such as axes and hatchets. Members of local militia were called to quell the slaughter, and the uprising ended two days after it began.

The rebellion had the effect opposite of what Turner had hoped. The great majority of African Americans who aided him were rounded up and executed, as were a few who had little or nothing to do with the incident. Turner himself fled but was captured two months later, given a brief trial, and also executed. And the fear that spread like fire among whites in the South led to

Nat Turner said that he had received several visions from God before the rebellion in 1831.

JOHN BROWN'S RAID

Another notable abolitionist protest occurred shortly before the outbreak of the Civil War. It was led by John Brown, a white man who was born in Connecticut in 1800. By the 1850s, he had become a devout antislavery activist who believed the only way for slaves to reach freedom was through armed warfare. To that end, he planned and led a raid on a military armory located in the town of Harpers Ferry, Virginia. He thought the weapons he would seize there would be used for future revolts.

The raid began on the night of October 16, 1859, and lasted for two days, after which Brown's band was put down by US marines, led by future Confederate general Robert E. Lee. Approximately half of Brown's men were killed, and another seven (including Brown himself) were captured and eventually executed. But perhaps the most profound effect of the raid was that news of the bloody affair increased tensions between North and South. This played a role in the election of Abraham Lincoln to the presidency, the secession of the Southern states, and the outbreak of the Civil War, culminating in the defeat of the South and the end of slavery.

new laws that forbade slaves from receiving educations, gathering in large groups, and accessing many other basic civil rights.

THE POWER OF LABOR UNIONS

The main focus of the second half of the 1800s was America's Reconstruction. This was the rebuilding of a unified United States in the aftermath of the Civil War (1861–1865). During this period, the US economy fluctuated tremendously, creating periods of great prosperity and equally great struggle.

One of the darkest economic downturns occurred in 1873. In the wake of the Civil War, there was a boom period during which money was poured into the expansion of the US railroad system. Between 1868 and 1873, roughly 33,000 miles (53,000 km) of track were laid around the country.[4] Unfortunately, the rail industry grew at a much greater rate than was sustainable. By the autumn of 1873, banks and other financial firms were failing, which set off a tremendous

Railroad strikes became a significant part of America's history during the late 1800s and early 1900s.

public panic. For the next four years, railroad workers looked on helplessly as their livelihoods deteriorated. Many were let go, and those who remained employed were forced to accept reductions in their pay. The first two rounds of pay reduction were met with great anger and resentment, but the third—applied in the summer of 1877—pushed workers beyond their limits.

THE GREAT RAILROAD STRIKE OF 1877

What would become known as the Great Railroad Strike of 1877 began on July 16, in the town of Martinsburg, West Virginia. After demanding that a third pay reduction be revoked to no avail, workers walked away from their posts and made certain all trains under their control were unable to move. The governor of West Virginia believed the strike could be easily ended by sending in militiamen. When the strikers still refused to return to work, the militia refused to use force against them.

Over the next few weeks, word of the Martinsburg workers' boldness inspired other railroad employees to do the same. Similar strikes followed in Maryland, New York, Pennsylvania, Missouri, and Illinois. In many instances, local militia also followed suit, refusing to harm workers with whom they sympathized. Workers in other industries, including coal miners in several Illinois towns, also walked off the job to show their support. The railroad strike succeeded in shutting down freight traffic intended to travel all over the nation.

Officials at various levels of government still refused to bend to the workers' demands. Instead, armed forces were sent to various sites. The confrontations quickly descended into violence, resulting in the widespread destruction of property, numerous injuries, and even some deaths.

The Great Railroad Strike of 1877 lasted for 45 days across multiple states.

In Maryland, a regiment of troops approached by an angry mob began firing their rifles and killed almost a dozen citizens. In Chicago, more than 5,000 militiamen were called to action, and street fights between militia, police, and rioters resulted in at least another 20 deaths. And in Pittsburgh, soldiers were attacked by a crowd throwing rocks and responded by killing 20 more.[5] In response, the city broke out in a surge of rioting that lasted more than a month. This resulted in almost a dozen more deaths and damage to millions of dollars' worth of property, including hundreds of engine and freight cars.

The Great Railroad Strike of 1877 did little to solve the problems that triggered it. Relations between workers and owners became more strained than ever. Workers then sought union-type representation and became better organized. In turn, owners made a greater effort to squash future attempts at unionization, going so far as to threaten or

SECOND STRIKE

The second major confrontation between railroad workers and owners came in May 1894, with the Pullman Strike. The name came from the Pullman Palace Car Company, which had cut workers' pay. The strike was very similar to the 1877 event, spurred largely by low wages and complaints of unfair treatment and substandard working conditions. This time, more than 250,000 railroad workers in more than 25 states were involved. Once again, rioting and military intervention resulted in numerous deaths and extensive property damage.

even fire those who were suspected of taking part in such activities. And states made sure their military units were better trained and equipped to handle future uprisings. Each side seemed determined to prepare itself for the next confrontation rather than avoid it.

THE FIGHT FOR IMPROVED WORKING CONDITIONS

Along with the battle for better pay in the late 1800s came the push for improved working conditions. By the time of Reconstruction following the Civil War, the United States had entered a period of rapid industrialization, and many jobs became more dangerous than ever. Machines were being substituted for hand tools, steam-powered engines for animals, and elevators for ladders. Other powerful technologies brought new and increased risks like never before.

The campaign for better working conditions had to be taken up piecemeal, and one of the first aspects pursued was shorter working hours. In some professions, a limit of eight hours per day was already supported by law. But in others, no such regulation was in place and ten or more hours were the norm. While workers understood that more hours meant more pay, it also meant an increase in on-the-job fatigue, which resulted in a greater chance of making a mistake that could lead to

THE LEGAL SIDE OF STRIKING

The legality of strikes has been a tricky issue in the United States for a very long time. Removing workers' right to strike would, in many ways, leave them at the mercy of their employers. On the other hand, there are many professions so critical to the daily flow of life that a strike would cause tremendous damage. Laws were passed in the 1930s that gave workers the right to both strike and join labor unions. And 1935's Wagner Act produced the National Labor Relations Board, a governmental agency whose mandate was to help solve management-labor issues in private industries. Following a period of labor unrest in the wake of World War II (1939–1945), the federal government passed the Taft-Hartley Act. This imposed limitations on strike-related activities, nearly preventing them altogether. Further complicating the issue are strike-related laws that exist in some states but not in others, and bans on striking in certain public-sector jobs, but not those in the private sector.

personal catastrophe. Additionally, more time at work meant less time with families at home.

In May 1886, workers organized widespread protests to demand an across-the-board rule for an eight-hour work day. These protests produced little in the way of immediate results—and in one case, they turned into tragedy. On May 3, in Milwaukee, Wisconsin, approximately 14,000 laborers gathered by an iron company's mill.[6] Businesses were forced to shut down because so many workers had walked off the job to take part in the protest.

In response, Governor Jeremiah Rusk sent in National Guard forces, who had the order to shoot if any of the workers attempted to enter the mill itself. Tensions rose over the course of that day and the next, and on the morning of May 5, some of the protesters approached the mill. Guardsmen fired into the crowd and killed seven people, including a boy who was just 13 years old. Although the incident sparked outrage among the working class around the nation, the eight-hour workday that the protesters had been seeking remained unresolved until well into the 1900s.

DISCUSSION STARTERS

- Consider Ona Judge. Is an act a protest if it only affects one person?

- If you were one of the railroad owners, what would you have done in the aftermath of the 1877 strike to make sure it didn't happen again?

- Do you believe striking should be forbidden by federal law? Why or why not?

CHAPTER 4

WOMEN'S SUFFRAGE

Two women campaigning for the right to vote
in Chicago, Illinois, in 1905

The 1900s was a time of significant change in the United
States. The degree of social upheaval during those hundred
years was truly remarkable, as was the frequency of
reactionary activity.

WOMEN TAKE A STAND

The role of women in US society has long been a topic of
importance with much disagreement. In the workplace,
women have rarely enjoyed the same privileges and rewards
as men. In the nation's earliest days following independence,

the great majority of politicians, business leaders, and landowners were men. Starting in the early 1800s, as the United States began to experience significant expansion and industrialization, scores of men began leaving their homes to work instead of farming. Women then were expected to adopt domestic roles for themselves, such as keeping the house and raising the children.

Even at this time, many women were frustrated with their limited citizenship. The United States was a society controlled by men, but some women were willing to take a stand. One of these trailblazers was Sojourner Truth. Truth was born a slave in 1797. She fled to freedom in 1826 after years of abuse at the hands of several different owners. At the time of her escape, she had five children, but only a daughter was with her. One of her sons had been sold into slavery in Alabama. That sale, however, was illegal, and Truth boldly took the man responsible to court. She won the case and got her son back, and she also made a mark in history as the first African-American woman to win a case of that nature against a white man.[1]

In July 1848, one of the first important public events regarding suffrage took place: a convention on women's rights was held in the New York town of Seneca Falls. It was organized by some of the leading feminists of the day,

Sojourner Truth was an important women's rights advocate, speaking at many conventions throughout her lifetime.

including Elizabeth Cady Stanton and Lucretia Mott. Over the course of two days, Stanton, Mott, and others discussed the role of women in society, particularly noting its shortcomings

ELIZABETH CADY STANTON

Stanton was born on November 12, 1815, in Johnstown, New York. As a young woman, Stanton received a formal education—which was still somewhat unusual for a woman at the time—and was an excellent student, winning numerous academic awards. She became actively involved in the women's rights movement in the 1840s, developing friendships with some of the leading feminists of the day. In 1868, she gave a speech in Washington, DC, that took direct aim at some of the failings of men. It included lines such as, "The male element is a destructive force, stern, selfish, aggrandizing [boasting], loving war, violence, conquest, acquisition, breeding in the material and moral world alike discord, disorder, disease, and death."[2] It is considered one of the most powerful moments in a long career of activism that included global travel, the writing of dozens of articles and speeches, and participation in numerous conventions and other meetings. Stanton passed away in October 1902, at the age of 86.

and their solutions.

One of the points that stirred tremendous reaction among the growing equal-rights movement was that of suffrage—the right for women to vote. The issues discussed at the Seneca Falls convention were eventually recorded in a document known as the Declaration of Sentiments. Its key points included women's desire to have a greater role in lawmaking, equality in citizenship, equality in property ownership, more employment opportunities, and avenues for pursuing upward social mobility.

The Declaration of Sentiments was eventually signed by 100 of the roughly 300 people in attendance, including 32 men. All the topics outlined in the declaration would soon receive increasing attention, and the Seneca convention inspired numerous others like it in the decades ahead.

SUFFRAGE MOVEMENT

By the 1870s, two separate suffrage organizations had taken root. The National Woman Suffrage Association was formed by Stanton along with the now-legendary Susan B. Anthony. The other group, the American Woman Suffrage Association, was launched by Massachusetts feminist Lucy Stone. The two groups joined in 1890 to create the National American Woman Suffrage Association.

Another major figure at this time was Ida B. Wells, who was born into slavery in Mississippi in 1862. She was involved in both African-American and women's rights activities, including the formation of a suffrage organization in Illinois in 1913. These women and scores of others rallied in an attempt to get the government to add an amendment to the Constitution entitling them to vote.

With little to show for these efforts beyond public support, a woman named Alice Paul formed an organization called the National Woman's Party (NWP). The NWP had the mandate to take more aggressive actions. When the United States got involved in World War I (1914–1918) in 1917, many women were expected to fill jobs traditionally reserved for men while the latter went overseas to fight. When women still weren't given the right to vote, Paul and the NWP began marching and picketing outside the White House in January 1917. Up to this point, the White House had never seen protesters

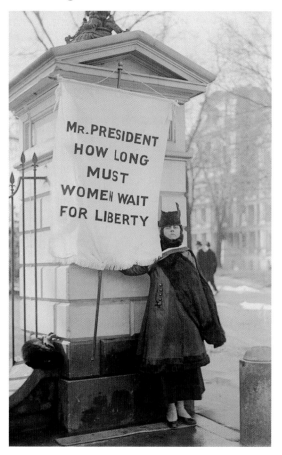

A woman protests outside the White House for women's rights in 1917.

before. Some people on the scene began abusing the protesters, destroying their banners and spitting on them. Police also asked the protesters to leave, and when they refused, they were arrested. Many were thrown in jail. While imprisoned, some went on a hunger strike, refusing to eat for weeks at a time. A Washington circuit court of appeals later ruled that their arrest and imprisonment violated their constitutional rights and were therefore illegal. The press made a big deal out of these proceedings, and public support for the suffrage movement became stronger than ever. As a result, laws were passed in many states finally giving women the right to vote. The Nineteenth Amendment to the Constitution, giving all women in the United States this right, passed in Congress on June 4, 1919. All states fully ratified it by August 18, 1920.

THE NINETEENTH AMENDMENT

The amendment to the US Constitution that finally broke down the barriers to women's suffrage was ratified on August 18, 1920. This amendment, the Constitution's nineteenth, was the result of a 70-year battle between the women's movement and the political powers in Washington. And there were plenty of defeats along the way. In 1878, for example, the National Woman Suffrage Association—formed by Elizabeth Cady Stanton and Susan B. Anthony in 1869—persuaded Congress to consider the amendment. Unfortunately, after the issue was studied and debated, the proposal was defeated. By the 1890s, however, women's suffrage organizations had successfully persuaded several states, including Wyoming, Colorado, Utah, and Ohio, to adopt provisions for women's voting. By 1918, President Woodrow Wilson gave his support to a suffrage amendment, which helped the Nineteenth Amendment pass in 1919 by a significant majority in both the House and the Senate.

The power and position of women in US society has improved since the 1960s. However, protest marches, lawsuits, politicking, and other activities continue. The pay gap, for example, is still an issue, with modern women earning approximately 80 percent of what male counterparts earn in the workplace.[3] While this is a leap from a generation ago, it is still far from equal. And for women of color, the situation is even worse. African-American women earn approximately 65 cents on the dollar, and Latinas earn approximately 58 cents on the dollar.[4]

Women are joining the modern feminist movement by the thousands. The Equal Rights Amendment (ERA) is a proposed addition to the Constitution that would specifically protect the rights of women against any type of sexual discrimination. It was first touted in 1923 and strongly advocated in the 1960s and 1970s, but by the early 1980s it had missed its deadline for ratification. Modern feminists have once again taken up the cause of seeing the ERA pass through Congress. Jessica Neuwirth, coauthor of the 2015 book *Equal Means Equal: Why the Time for an Equal Rights Amendment Is Now*, told CNN, "Surely with social media and the new generation of women and men who do not believe in second-class citizenship for women, we can get the ERA across the finish line and put it in the Constitution where it belongs."[5]

IT'S 2017 EQUALITY HURTS ♀ NO ONE!!

@woman_kind   #WhyIMarch

WOMEN'S MOVEMENT CONTINUES

While the central focus of the women's movement from the mid-1800s to the early 1900s was suffrage, a much wider range of issues flowed out of feminist activism in the 1960s. This was a time when topics such as sexuality, gender equality in the workplace, women's roles at home, and domestic violence moved to the fore. As the postwar era merged into the 1960s, many women decided they liked the idea of a career beyond motherhood and domesticity. However, they discovered the average woman's salary was only approximately 60 percent of that earned by men in similar positions.[6] The National Organization for Women formed in 1966. This plus the rise of major feminist figures, such as Gloria Steinem and Betty Friedan, paved the way for a movement that would forever redefine the relationship between men and women in America. This movement is still on the forefront of America's most important issues today.

DISCUSSION STARTERS

- Why do you think it has taken so long for women's rights to be supported?
- What issues do you feel women should still be protesting today?

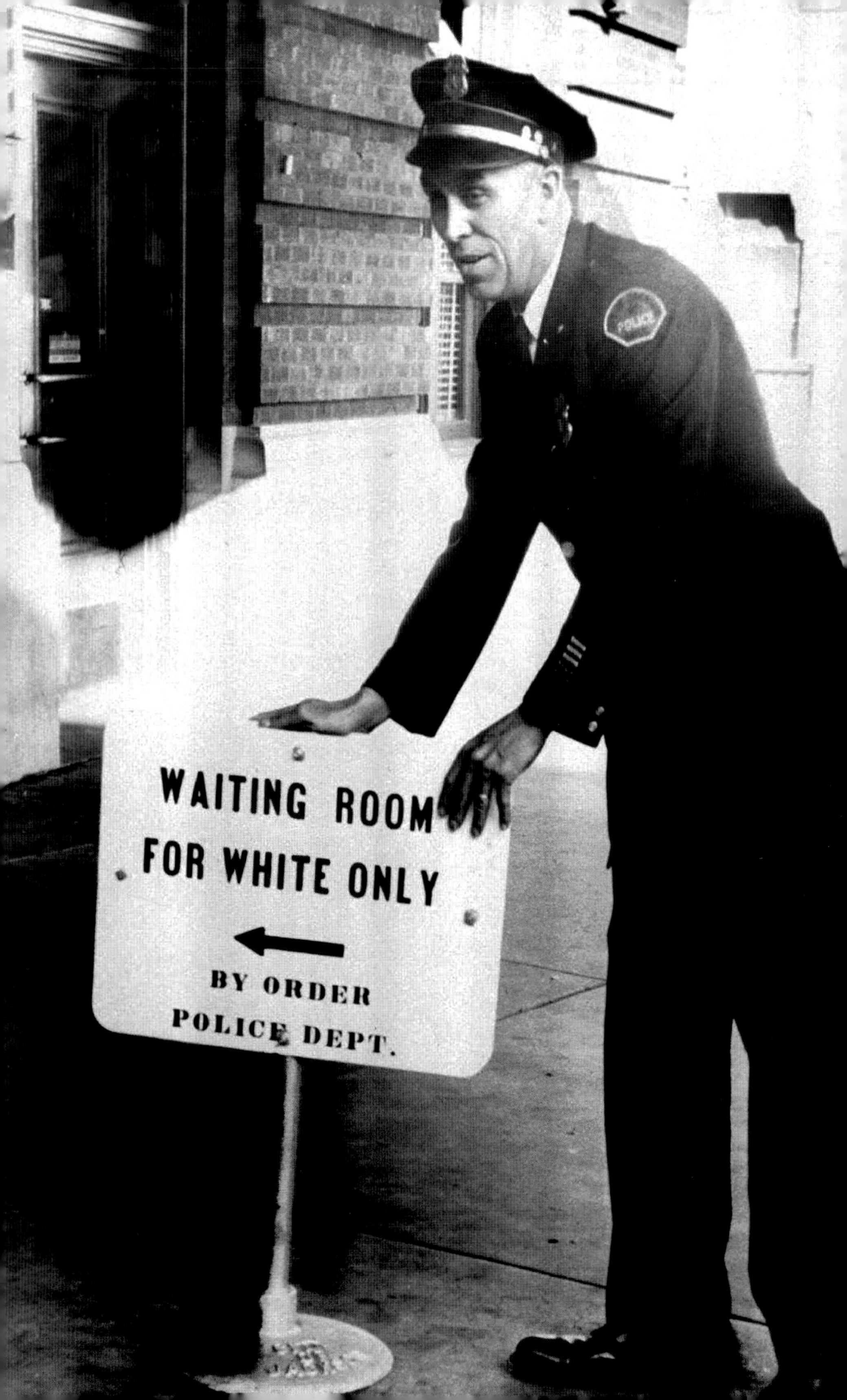
WAITING ROOM
FOR WHITE ONLY
BY ORDER
POLICE DEPT.
POLICE

THE CIVIL RIGHTS MOVEMENT

Minority rights have always been a hot-button issue in the United States. Abraham Lincoln issued the Emancipation Proclamation through executive order in 1863. Then he shepherded the passage of the Thirteenth Amendment to the Constitution and thus abolished slavery permanently. Since then, the struggle for social equality among African Americans has been tremendous. Despite gaining their freedom following the Civil War, they were hardly treated equally. In the years following World War II, African Americans were still not treated fairly by white people.

The police enforced segregation laws at a Mississippi railroad station in 1956 after the station had removed all segregation signs.

In some parts of the country, the average black citizen had to endure the daily humiliation of being refused service at gas stations, not being allowed to purchase goods at some supermarkets, or being unable to attend good schools. Special regulations known as Jim Crow laws were put in place to keep blacks away from whites, following what was supposed to be a "separate but equal" approach. But rare was the instance when a store or school or public restroom designated for African Americans was truly equal to the facilities provided for whites.

PLESSY V. FERGUSON

The separate-but-equal philosophy was couched in the broader concept of segregation. Through its simplest definition, this meant that whites and blacks could live in the same area as long as they were kept separate in all meaningful respects. This notion was fully supported by the Supreme Court at one point, most notably in a landmark case known as *Plessy v. Ferguson*. It began with an incident in 1892 involving Homer Plessy, a mixed-race man in Louisiana, who tried to take a seat in a train car intended only for whites. He was arrested, and when he took the case to court, the Louisiana judge ruled against him. Plessy's lawyers then brought the case all the way to the US Supreme Court in 1896. Plessy once again found himself on the losing side—and the court's decision strengthened segregation.

START OF A MOVEMENT

What finally overturned the separate-but-equal concept—and, in turn, helped launch the historic civil rights movement of the mid-1900s—was a landmark case, *Brown v. Board of Education*. The case argued, in essence, that white schools were demonstrably superior to black schools in virtually every respect: better teachers, better facilities, better books, and so on. The Supreme Court agreed in a unanimous decision, and in May 1954, segregation was ruled unconstitutional.

Many people around the country were unhappy with the implications of the decision. Many political leaders on various levels—local, county, and state—refused to support or enforce any action that led to integration. This continued resistance drove many in the African-American community and their white allies to mobilize and protest more vigorously than they ever had before.

THE MONTGOMERY BUS BOYCOTT

Protest activity during the civil rights movement took on many forms, from relatively passive to outright hostile and violent. One of the most famous examples of the former was the Montgomery bus boycott.

The incident that sparked the boycott involved an African-American woman named Rosa Parks. Parks lived and worked in Montgomery, Alabama. On December 1, 1955, while she was sitting on a crowded bus, a white man got on. The bus driver ordered Parks to give up her seat on the bus to the man,

Rosa Parks at her arrest in 1955

but she refused. She was eventually arrested and charged, which sparked outrage among the local black community.

One of the leaders of the burgeoning civil rights movement at this time was Dr. Martin Luther King Jr. A Baptist minister from Georgia, King's oratorical skills were so powerful and persuasive that he quickly became one of the movement's guiding lights. He knew how important it was to stand up for his beliefs, once saying that "Every man of humane convictions must decide on the protest that best suits his convictions, but we must all protest."[1] King then helped plan and carry out a boycott of the Montgomery busing system, and for the next year, African Americans in the area refused to ride. Since the buses needed the money from their patronage to function, this put a tremendous strain on their operations. In June, the federal court in Montgomery ruled that segregation on the city's buses did, in fact, violate the Fourteenth Amendment of the Constitution, which forbids states from denying anyone "life, liberty, or property, without due process of law." The city attempted to appeal the case by taking it all the way to the Supreme Court. The Supreme Court announced in December 1956 that it agreed with the lower court's decision, and all buses were ordered desegregated. After 381 days of boycotting, the African-American community of Montgomery got what it wanted—and made history in the process.[2]

THE MARTIN LUTHER KING JR. RIOTS OF 1968

By 1968, King had become one of the most important figures in the movement. His speeches were the stuff of legend, but his decidedly nonviolent protesting strategy also shook the movement. He spoke often of how love rather than hatred would eventually conquer racism. This positive approach made it difficult for others to feel hostile toward him.

But King could not cure all hatred. King was shot dead on April 4, 1968, in Memphis, Tennessee, by James Earl Ray, a white man on the run after escaping from prison in Missouri the previous year. News of King's death spread rapidly, and

Several buildings were burnt down in Chicago, Illinois, during riots following King's assassination in 1968.

rioting soon broke out all around the country. This was not the first time riots had occurred over racial tension. During the previous summer of 1967, dubbed "the long, hot summer," riots occurred across the country over the continual mistreatment of African Americans. Most of the riots occurred in major cities, including Chicago, Illinois; Detroit, Michigan; and Washington, DC. The majority of the participants were African American. The protests against King's death spanned over 125 cities and in some areas

THE CIVIL RIGHTS ACTS OF 1964 AND 1968

The Civil Rights Act of 1964 attempted to eradicate the plague of racial discrimination in numerous forms, including voter registration, employment policy, and education. A lesser-known progression of the act was the Civil Rights Act of 1968, also known as the Fair Housing Act. It specifically protected people from being kept out of certain living spaces because of their race, religion, or ethnicity. This included the sale of living quarters, which covered related issues such as ability to secure a mortgage or other financial assistance. Like the earlier act, it was signed into law by President Lyndon B. Johnson, just days after the MLK riots began. Some historians believe Johnson and others took this measure to calm the rioters and the black community as a whole, as the proposal for the act had been introduced into Congress more than a year earlier and had been dragging through congressional process prior to King's assassination.

PERSPECTIVES
1960s SIT-INS

One of the more popular forms of passive protest during the 1950s and 1960s was known as the "sit-in," in which protesters would occupy a certain space where they otherwise might not be allowed. Among those were the historic lunch counter sit-ins that took place in Greensboro, North Carolina, in 1960.

Four African-American college students, inspired by Martin Luther King Jr., decided to take action against a local Woolworth department store, which practiced segregationist policies. On February 1, they walked in, purchased some items, and then sat down at the store's lunch counter and ordered coffee. The lunch counter was segregated, and the four were sitting at the whites-only section. They were refused service and told to leave, but they remained until closing. The next day, they were joined by approximately 20 more students. On the third day, the number rose to 60. On the fourth, there were more than 300.[3]

By the summer, with losses from the sit-ins mounting fast, the Greensboro Woolworth decided to change its policy and began serving African-American customers. Perhaps even more importantly, the actions of the four students—who became known as the Greensboro Four—brought national attention to segregation.

continued for a full week. President Lyndon Johnson urged local and state authorities to use as little force as possible, but in some cases this advice was either ignored or deemed impossible. Johnson quickly realized he had little choice but to call for military deployment, and the army and the National Guard were soon racing to the worst areas of the turmoil.

In the aftermath of the riots, the cost in terms of both property and human life was startling. Dozens of people lost their lives, thousands more were injured, and urban areas sustained losses in the hundreds of millions of dollars. This also marked the end of King's approach to racial discrimination, which was founded on the notion of nonviolent behavior. There were lasting effects, too, including a drive among whites to move out of areas where African Americans had begun to move in, a phenomenon later dubbed "white flight."[4]

DISCUSSION STARTERS

- What issues or movements do you think would be important to Martin Luther King Jr. if he were still alive today?

- Do you see any ongoing examples of segregation in society today? If so, what do you think should be done about them?

CHAPTER 6

WAR PROTESTS

VIETNAM AND
S AT HOME!

One protest against the Vietnam War took place in 1968 and included the first woman ever elected to Congress, Jeannette Rankin, *fourth from right.*

Along with the civil rights movement, the 1960s also saw numerous protests against US involvement in war. Social sentiment came to a boil over the Vietnam War (1954–1975).

Tensions between the United States and Vietnam had been brewing since the 1910s, starting with President Woodrow Wilson's refusal to support Vietnam's efforts to break free of French control. By the mid-1950s, the French had been driven out and the nation began to divide into two separate regions, north and south. North Vietnam eventually came under the control of a communist government guided

THE GULF OF TONKIN INCIDENT

One of the elements critical to the American public's eventual distrust of its government involved what became known as the Gulf of Tonkin incident. It occurred between US and Vietnamese forces off the coasts of Vietnam and China in 1964. The official story was that Vietnamese torpedo boats attacked US ships and thus President Johnson felt obliged to take action against Vietnam. Antiwar activists responded with a campaign to find out whether this incident really occurred as described, or whether it was invented to justify an increase in US involvement in the conflict. The latter proved true, and the damage to the government's credibility led to considerable anger— and powerful motivation for the antiwar movement.

by revolutionary leader Hồ Chí Minh. South Vietnam adopted a more moderate, socialist system under the leadership of Ngô Dình Diệm.

By the early 1960s, Minh's government was threatening to invade South Vietnam and surrounding nations, such as Laos. This came at a time when the relationship between the capitalist United States and the communist Soviet Union was at its most antagonistic. In May 1961, President John F. Kennedy began sending US troops into South Vietnam to help its military keep North Vietnam's forces at bay and, in turn, stem the spread of communism.

Despite reassurances that US involvement in the North–South Vietnam conflict would be minimal, large numbers of troops were sent there by the mid-1960s under President Johnson. And although the United States had played a critical role in the victories of World War I and World War II, the battles in Vietnam did not run as smoothly. Young American men died by the thousands. Many had been drafted into the military through a system that was deemed corrupt. The system was tilted to favor exceptions for children of the wealthy while

A 1965 law made it illegal to burn draft cards. Many who did served time in prison, including David Paul O'Brien, *left*, who later took the case to court, arguing that his arrest violated his free speech rights.

enlisting a disproportionately large number of those from lower- and middle-class families. While the US government attempted to paint a positive picture of the war's progress, unprecedented coverage of the war through television and other media outlets told a very different story. This led people to protest.

EARLY PROTESTS

Dedicated attempts to protest against the Vietnam War began in earnest around 1964. These protests were relatively peaceful and passive, including the public burning of draft cards and demonstrations involving several hundred people at a time. Then 1965 saw a marked increase in protest activity, ranging from more marches to card-burning incidents. There was also an increase in the number of participants, such as a pair of marches in Washington, DC—one on April 17, the other on November 27—that involved approximately 25,000 and 30,000 people respectively.[1]

It's important to note that the majority of people who took part in these early demonstrations did not have the support of most Americans. Early resisters of the Vietnam War were often viewed negatively, as antiestablishment types, and given nicknames such as "peaceniks" and "hippies." Gallup polls taken in 1965 clearly indicated that many Americans still believed the conflict in Vietnam was just, and thus so were the actions taken by the government. For example, a Gallup poll in May showed that just under half of all respondents supported the war, whereas only a little more than a quarter were against it.[2] Much of the public felt the activists had no real right to protest the matter, and some resisters were openly mistreated as they did so. With the public's support, President Johnson sent more than 200,000 more troops into Vietnam in November of that year.[3]

TINKER V. DES MOINES

One landmark case that cemented the right to protest in America was that of *Tinker v. Des Moines Independent Community School District*. In 1969, five students at a public high school in Des Moines, Iowa, planned to protest the Vietnam War by wearing black bands around their arms. This protest was intended to be silent and was not going to disrupt the school day. The principal, however, found out what the students were planning to do and banned students from wearing the armbands. But the students wore the armbands to school anyway. The students were asked to take the bands off, and when they refused, they were suspended from school. The students and their parents then sued the school, stating the suspension was a violation of the students' free speech rights. Four years later, the court decided that the students did in fact have every right to protest by wearing the armbands, saying, "In wearing armbands, the petitioners were quiet and passive. They were not disruptive, and did not impinge upon the rights of others. In these circumstances, their conduct was within the protection of the Free Speech Clause of the First Amendment."[4]

THE TIDE TURNS

From 1966 onward, public opinion of the Vietnam War began to change, and support for Johnson and his administration deteriorated, for multiple reasons. For one, reports began reaching the US media that the war was not going quite as well as the government had been claiming, and this led to an unprecedented degree of mistrust in the government. Second, the timeline for the war's end kept changing, making it difficult for Americans to trust that an end would indeed come. Also, the casualty count was rising rapidly, with most of the dead being very young men. The average age of a US soldier in Vietnam was 19.[5] The names of the dead were being printed in local newspapers, and the sense of war glory that had been such an important factor in public support of World Wars I and II began to fade as news of the true ugliness of such conflicts replaced it. This included reports of atrocities, such as the My Lai massacre of March 16, 1968, in which US troops killed approximately 500 unarmed civilians in South Vietnam, including women, children, and even infants.[6]

All of the above resulted in a much broader protest movement, with participation growing well beyond the peaceniks and hippies. By the late 1960s, it included people of all ages, races, genders, and faiths. Mothers, teachers and other academics, religious leaders, white-collar professionals, journalists and others in the media, and in some cases even veterans of past wars joined the movement, as did a few politicians. New pacifist organizations were being formed, and existing ones, such as Students for a Democratic Society and the Women's International League for Peace and Freedom,

The National Moratorium on October 15, 1969, is believed to have been the largest US protest, with an estimated two million people gathering across the country to protest the Vietnam War.

found new cause in the antiwar effort. By mid-1968, polls showed a clear majority of Americans believed involvement in the war had been a mistake.

Naturally, the protesting continued. One of the most notable events occurred in Washington, DC, on November 15, 1969, when roughly 500,000 demonstrators gathered. With the support of the nation behind them, protesters felt more vindicated in their right to speak out than ever before.

It reached a point where the only factions who stood against the protesters were civil authorities such as local police, plus federal forces such as the National Guard. But most Vietnam War protests were peaceful. Regardless of the protesters' legal right to demonstrate peacefully, some events ended with violence and bloodshed.

ATTEMPTS TO CIRCUMVENT THE RIGHT TO PROTEST

Some of the greatest tension that existed during the protests of the 1960s was between protesters and law enforcement. While the right to peaceful protesting was protected by the Constitution, police in some areas, either acting on their own behalf or at the direction of other local authorities, found ways to circumvent protesting rights and strike back against activists. One common practice was to have police incite a protesting crowd into violence, thus giving themselves the right to use force. Entrapment was another approach whereby drugs or other illegal substances were planted on protesters, who could then be arrested on "legitimate" grounds.

Some of the most famous were the riots that broke out in Chicago during the 1968 Democratic National Convention, which involved approximately 10,000 protesters who were eventually assaulted by police with mace and billy clubs.[7] Much of this was broadcast live on television, which resulted in public outcry as well as a powerful impact on the 1968 elections.

Although vigorous public opposition to the Vietnam War lasted through the 1960s and into the 1970s, US involvement did not end until 1973. By that time, US deaths numbered more than 58,000.[8] The average person's opinion on the right to protest government irresponsibility and deceit was at an all-time high. The relationship between the American people and their government would never be the same.

DISCUSSION STARTERS

- Would your position on the Vietnam War be different if a member of your family was a soldier fighting in Vietnam and was for the war rather than against it?

- If you were against the Vietnam War in the early 1960s when most Americans were still for it, would you have taken part in any public protests? Why or why not?

- What could the US government have done in the aftermath of the Vietnam War to restore the public's trust and rebuild the public's confidence in the government?

CHAPTER 7

PROTESTING IN THE DIGITAL AGE

During the Occupy Wall Street movement, this reporter live streamed the story, so people who weren't there could see exactly what was going on.

Despite the new millennium and the election of the United States' first African-American president in 2008, there is a sense of social injustice in the air. Appropriately called the Digital Age, recent years have seen Internet and cell phone communication technology become powerful instruments in our society. These tools have afforded protesters greater opportunities to connect and engage than at any other time in history.

SLAYING THE DRAGONS
OF BIG BUSINESS

Issues stemming from excessive corporate influence have always sparked strong reactions in the United States. In a system built on a free-market economy and capitalism, large

Despite the pouring rain, the Occupy Wall Street protesters continued.

businesses often cross the lines of acceptable moral behavior. These businesses often become so disproportionately powerful that their profit-driven actions can cause harm to ordinary citizens.

One of the most significant examples of protest against this phenomenon in recent times was the Occupy Wall Street movement. The 2007–2008 financial crisis was a key inspiration for the movement. This financial crash was triggered in large part by several powerful banking and investment institutions that became involved with high-risk endeavors. A string of bad losses eventually caused the collapse of several firms and the near collapse of the global financial system, dragging the country into one of the most damaging and painful recessions in history. It was considered by most experts to be the worst since the Great Depression of the 1930s.

Millions of people were enraged when many of the failed institutions were bailed out by the US government. Virtually no individuals were held accountable for their roles in the disaster. Large numbers of ordinary citizens lost their jobs and their savings. By 2012, many of the bailed-out firms had regained their former strength. Yet ordinary people continued to suffer the aftereffects of the firms' actions. Many experienced prolonged unemployment, which resulted in the loss of homes, cars, and other personal property.

In early 2011, a Canadian publication called *Adbusters* proposed a protest movement staged in the United States called the "Million Man March on Wall Street." It was promoted as a peaceful protest, an outlet for those who were upset that there had been no convictions for the people responsible for the "Great Recession." They wanted to protest the power US corporations had over lawmakers, as well as the enormous gap between the super-wealthy and everyone else. The latter became the inspiration for one of the central slogans of the movement: "We are the 99%." This referred to the percentage of the population who were not among the wealthiest citizens in the country, who are also known as the top 1 percent.

The first of the Occupy Wall Street protests began on September 17, 2011, when approximately 1,000 people gathered at New York's Zuccotti Park.[1] Over the next few

THE COST OF PROTESTING

Since the majority of OWS activists who took part in the 2011 protests remained on the Zuccotti Park property for long periods, someone had to cover the related costs of them being there. Outside donors made some contributions, with the average amount being $22 and the total donations reaching approximately $700,000.[2] The day-to-day expenses included food and drink for the participants, transportation for those who didn't stay overnight (such as bus and subway tickets), tech equipment that allowed them to get on their computers and use the Internet, medical aid, and bail money for protesters who were arrested.

days, the media spread reports of the movement around the country. Approximately a month later, President Barack Obama openly expressed support for the protesters.

Finally, on November 15, police informed the protesters that they had to leave. When the protesters refused, New York City police forcibly evicted them from Zuccotti Park. These actions were within New York law. Nevertheless, new protests broke out in other locations around the city, involving nearly 30,000 people.[3] Similar protests began to occur around the nation, at which point a coherent message clearly emerged— that income inequality was worse than ever.

The topic of income inequality has become part of the national mind-set, and this raised awareness has had a lasting effect throughout society. Income inequality's effect on social class has become a common talking point in political debates. Similarly, since many of the participants in the Occupy Wall Street movement were young people with college educations, the heavy debt burdens they carried from their college costs have also become a major political issue. In turn, this spurred efforts to drive college costs down or find more manageable ways to reduce student debt.

Even though Clinton won the popular vote in the 2016 election, Trump won by securing enough votes in the Electoral College.

THE "DUMP TRUMP" CAMPAIGN

Politically motivated protest activity is nothing new in the United States, but the angry reaction to the election of Donald Trump before he even set foot in the Oval Office was relatively unusual.

Trump's rise to the presidency was anything but orthodox.
Born in Queens, New York, in 1946, he spent the majority
of his adult years working as a real-estate developer. As his
career progressed, his interests veered away from real estate.
He was once owner of the New Jersey Generals football team.

He authored a best-selling, semiautobiographical book. He was also the host of the hit television show *The Apprentice* from 2004 to 2015. And while he had dealt with many politicians over the years, he had never held any political office. Regardless, he plowed through a field of 16 other candidates to earn the Republican Party's nomination. Then Trump beat former first lady and secretary of state Hillary Clinton to win the presidency in November 2016.

It wasn't just Trump's stunning upset win that set off protesters by the millions around the nation. It was also the

One of the most popular protest slogans after Donald Trump's election was "Not My President."

tactics he used to secure his victory. He used language that was offensive to many. He openly insulted decorated war heroes. He taunted Clinton with the fact that her husband, former president Bill Clinton, had had multiple affairs. He insulted other politicians who supported Clinton. And he was even caught on videotape bragging about incidents of sexual assault he said he'd committed against various women.

Numerous protests had already taken place during Trump rallies at various stops along his campaign trail. But with so much negativity stacked against him, most people believed Clinton would easily carry the election. When the ballots were counted and Trump was declared the winner instead, the reaction was one of sheer outrage, and the protesting became more dramatic than ever.

Immediately after the election, organized activities broke out in major cities all across the country and even in other countries. In some US cities, these protests sometimes turned into all-out riots. In Oakland, California, for example, rioting lasted for more than three days, involved more than 7,000 people, and resulted in 30 arrests.[4] Many of the marches in other areas focused on issues the protesters felt would be under direct threat by a Trump presidency, such as the rights of immigrants, the LGBT community, and women. Experts on social activism have also noted that while many of the people involved were veterans of other protests, a larger-than-normal percentage were first-timers.

Also unusual was the fact that the protesting continued well after Trump was sworn into office. Many protests arose in immediate reaction to specific measures Trump took in office. For example, on January 27, 2017—just one week after beginning his presidency—Trump signed Executive Order 13769, also known as the travel ban, which prevented people from certain countries from entering the United States. People around the world were furious with the decision.

Some protest activities during Trump's campaign and election had been violent. However, no protest was as violent as what happened in Charlottesville, Virginia. On August 12, 2017, hundreds of white supremacists gathered at Emancipation Park. They were protesting the planned removal of a statue of Confederate general Robert E. Lee. In return, hundreds of counterprotesters, including members of Black Lives Matter, gathered to object to their behavior. Tensions were incredibly high and soon fights broke out between the two sides. As if that wasn't bad enough, later that day, a man purposefully drove his car into a crowd of the counterprotesters, killing one woman and injuring dozens of others. People across the country were horrified.

President Trump was later criticized for his response to the tragedy. While he condemned the behavior that happened in Charlottesville, many were outraged that he failed to rebuke the white supremacists themselves. The event left Americans confused and frustrated, wondering if the nation was perhaps moving backward in its ways.

Due to the rise in protests since Trump's presidency, Republican lawmakers started to push various bills aiming to put restrictions on the right to protest altogether. As of September 2017, at least six state legislatures have created bills that put limitations on anything from trespassing to loitering. Whether these bills will pass in the future and spread to other states is yet to be determined.

DISCUSSION STARTERS

- The Occupy Wall Street protesters in Zuccotti Park were demonstrating on private property. If Occupy protesters wanted to do this on land that you owned, would you allow it? Why or why not?

- What kind of activities do you feel are appropriate when protesting the policies of a US president, and what kind do you feel are not?

- The white supremacists in Charlottesville were protesting the removal of Confederate statues. Do you think that all statues honoring those from the Confederacy should be removed? Why or why not?

CHAPTER 8

THE RESULTS

On June 16, 2017, protesters in Minneapolis, Minnesota, blocked traffic on a highway to protest police brutality in the state.

People may ask whether protesting really makes a difference. There are countless examples throughout history of protesters failing to reach their objectives, which in turn seems to imply that their efforts were wasted. But there are also examples of protest efforts that had a metaphorically ground-shaking effect, not only by addressing an important issue of the day but also by altering the course of history in the aftermath.

THE VALUE OF CALM

It is impossible to precisely quantify the effects of any kind of protest. If a government changes a policy to be more environmentally friendly, or a corporation reworks the pricing structure on products in order to benefit the consumer, how can that be proven as a direct response to a gesture of protest? The situation is rarely so black and white.

There is, however, sufficient evidence that some protesting methods work better than others. For example, those that are conducted in a peaceful, levelheaded manner seem to elicit a greater response than those that rely on violence or other forms of aggression. Even if the

WHEN THINGS GET OUT OF HAND

Sometimes a large crowd can turn ugly, and in such cases law enforcement agencies have two basic approaches to quelling a riot: passive and aggressive. With the passive approach, they attempt to contain and, in a sense, control the rioters until their rage is exhausted. One of its advantages is that fewer people will be harmed in the long run. For example, police will surround a riot zone to keep it from spreading, but they do not engage the rioters face-to-face unless absolutely necessary. An aggressive strategy involves officers essentially becoming involved in the riot itself, putting themselves in harm's way as they try to squelch all violent activity. Tools at their disposal include nightsticks, trained dogs, various sprays and gases, and, as a last resort, heavier weaponry, such as handguns and rifles.

cause is just and the objectives reasonable and relatable, the public rarely seems to exhibit much sympathy for protesters who resort to destruction and injury.

BEING CLEAR

It is also important that protesters use solid evidence to get their message across. If protesters organize in such a way that their complaints and goals are clear, it is that much easier for people to understand them. This effort is further aided by sharing solid evidence that supports their cause. So, overall, smart communication is key. To that end, the most effective protests are those that have just one or two people at the forefront to act as the messenger. Activists who have taken the

THE IMPORTANCE OF CLEAR LEADERSHIP

While the Occupy Wall Street protests had a lasting effect on US society, many historians believe, in hindsight, that one of the reasons they didn't have an even greater impact was due to a lack of clear leadership. Some of the most successful protest movements in the past had at least one person who was looked upon as the leader, if not logistically then certainly spiritually. For example, while Rosa Parks did not lead the Montgomery bus boycott per se, it was her figure and her story that inspired the boycott. Similarly, Gloria Steinem has long been viewed as one of the guiding lights of the feminist movement. But who filled this role for Occupy Wall Street? Since that question was never really answered, the public was unable to look to a single person or a small group to act as the conduit for conveying the movement's central message.

time to think these things through will be regarded with greater respect and taken more seriously.

SIZE MAKES A DIFFERENCE

A long-pondered question among protesters was whether the number of people who showed up had any direct effect on the result. In 2011, four economists from Harvard University and Stockholm University undertook an intriguing study in an attempt to come up with an answer.

After the financial crash of 2008, the Tea Party political movement emerged. One of its goals was to protest what members considered excessive taxation and spending by the Obama administration. To further this effort, they undertook what became known as the Tax Day rallies. On April 15, 2009, at numerous locations around the country, people were encouraged to gather to voice their opposition to tax increases and wasteful government spending. It is believed that anywhere from 450,000 to 800,000 people showed up in total, at nearly 500 different locations.[1]

The study team discovered something interesting: in areas where it rained, the turnout was lower by at least half, and more in some places. This part of the research wasn't surprising, since most people don't care to stand out in the rain. What was surprising was that in the areas where

During the Tax Day rallies, certain Tea Party members had written on their signs that Tea stood for "Taxed Enough Already."

turnout was highest, the elected representatives took a more conservative stance on the tax-and-spend issues when it was time for them to vote. Furthermore, in those same high-turnout areas, Republican candidates enjoyed a higher number of votes during the next election cycle. And it wasn't a single protest that drove these differences, but rather the lasting impression it had on the people in those areas. The larger the crowd, the greater the effect.

PERSISTENCE

A final factor in getting results through protest is persistence. Studies have shown that protest movements that fizzle within a relatively short time are perceived as being built on half-hearted conviction in the first place.

The movement toward African-American equality in the United States is a lesson in the value of staying the course. African Americans and their supporters have kept fighting the same fight and making the same demands for many decades. As a result, it is impossible to doubt the conviction that drives the African-American cause, and that fact makes their movement all the more formidable and productive. In the 2000s, for example, the most powerful impact being made by the African-American community is likely through Black Lives Matter. This movement was created in 2012 and has grown significantly since, shedding light on the injustice of African Americans killed during disputes with the police.

The real value in persistence lies in the underlying message being sent to the wider public: that the objectives are worth fighting for. The message then for those who stand opposed is that those who have accepted the task of

Black Lives Matter first started as a hashtag online and quickly grew into a global movement. Raising awareness is just one way to bring justice.

protesting have no intention of backing down. When that kind of determination is employed, protesting has the ability to change the world.

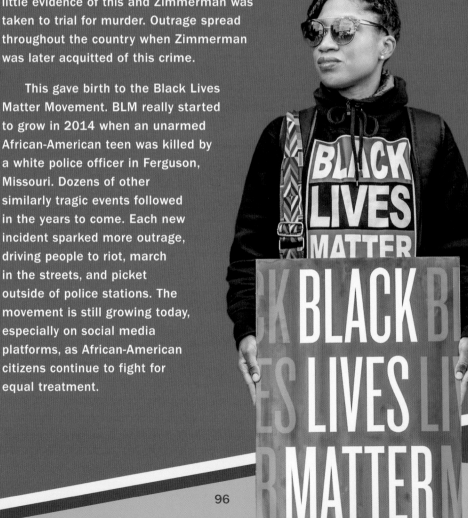

PERSPECTIVES
BLACK LIVES MATTER

On February 26, 2012, 17-year-old Trayvon Martin was walking home after a visit to a gas station in Sarasota, Florida. On his way home, a man named George Zimmerman, who was part of the neighborhood watch program, started following Martin, later saying that he looked "suspicious."[2] What exactly happened next is still unclear. Zimmerman and Martin appeared to have gotten into a scuffle, which resulted in Zimmerman shooting Martin in the chest and killing him. Zimmerman said he was acting in self-defense. However, the police found little evidence of this and Zimmerman was taken to trial for murder. Outrage spread throughout the country when Zimmerman was later acquitted of this crime.

This gave birth to the Black Lives Matter Movement. BLM really started to grow in 2014 when an unarmed African-American teen was killed by a white police officer in Ferguson, Missouri. Dozens of other similarly tragic events followed in the years to come. Each new incident sparked more outrage, driving people to riot, march in the streets, and picket outside of police stations. The movement is still growing today, especially on social media platforms, as African-American citizens continue to fight for equal treatment.

Ultimately, Americans have had a long history of standing up for what they believe in and standing against what they think is wrong. It is an essence of the American identity. As President Barack Obama said in 2014, "Let us remember we are all part of one American family. We are united in common values, and that includes belief in equality under the law, basic respect for public order, and the right of peaceful protest."[3]

DISCUSSION STARTERS

- Do you feel there is any issue so important that it's worth dying for? If so, what?

- Which protest discussed in this book do you feel was the most effective, and why?

- What issues that are important right now do you feel need more protesting than they are already receiving?

- Do you believe the human race can reach a point where protesting will no longer be necessary?

TIMELINE

1619
Polish craftsmen strike in Jamestown, Virginia, until they are given the right to vote. It is the first strike in the United States.

1773
At the height of tension between the colonists and the British government, an angry group of demonstrators boards a ship in Boston Harbor and destroys almost 350 chests of tea.

1831
Nat Turner's slave rebellion takes place in Virginia. Turner and his men slaughter many white slave owners before the rebellion is quelled.

1861
The Civil War begins. It is fought between the Southern and Northern states, with the issue of slavery at the center.

1877
Strikes are held in many places across the nation to protest continually reduced pay for railroad workers.

1894
Another strike by railroad workers begins in Chicago. It is called the Pullman Strike because it involves the workers on one side of the issue and the Pullman Company on the other.

1917
Alice Paul and her National Women's Party begin marching and picketing outside the White House in support of women's suffrage.

1955
The Montgomery bus boycott begins in response to the arrest of Rosa Parks, who refused to give her seat on a crowded bus to a white man.

1968

Riots occur in many cities throughout the nation in the wake of the assassination of Martin Luther King Jr. on April 4.

1970

Four students are killed by National Guard forces at Kent State University in Ohio during a protest against the Vietnam War. Two of the victims were not part of the protest activities.

2011

The Occupy Wall Street protests begin in New York City to oppose growing income equality in the United States.

2012

Black Lives Matter is started after the shooting of a 17-year-old African-American teen by a white man. This launches a movement that continues to grow after multiple unjust killings of African Americans.

2016-2017

Numerous protests occur—some turning violent—over the campaign and then presidency of Donald Trump.

ESSENTIAL FACTS

THE RIGHT TO PROTEST

The First Amendment to the Constitution guarantees "the right of the people peaceably to assemble, and to petition the government for a redress of grievances."

LIMITATIONS

Americans have the right to gather together to express their beliefs and opinions and to protest any issue they see fit. However, in doing so, Americans cannot disturb the peace, become violent, or destroy public property.

KEY PLAYERS

- Polish craftsmen staged the first worker's strike in America in Jamestown, Virginia, in 1619.

- Early American colonists staged one of the most significant protests in American history by leaving Great Britain and forming their own country. This revolution and the events leading up to it involved multiple protests, including the Boston Tea Party.

- Elizabeth Cady Stanton formed the National Woman Suffrage Association, a group that helped the women's movement take hold through many forms of protests and helped gain the right to vote for women.

- Rosa Parks sparked an extremely influential form of protesting when she refused to give up her bus seat for a white man in 1955, which led to the Montgomery bus boycotts (just one of many boycotts that occurred during the civil rights movement).

KEY PERSPECTIVES

- If Americans are feeling like their rights are being taken away, their voices are being ignored, or that they have been treated unjustly, they have the right to gather together and express their opinions on the matter.

- There are many ways people can protest, including boycotts, picketing, and vigils.

- Peaceful and passive protests have had the most positive influence throughout American history.

- It's important that each protest has a clear objective, a leader, and a solution in mind in order to get the best outcome.

QUOTE

"Every man of humane convictions must decide on the protest that best suits his convictions, but we must all protest."

— *Dr. Martin Luther King Jr.*

GLOSSARY

ACTIVISM
Taking part in vigorous campaigns to bring about political or social change.

BOYCOTT
To refuse to have dealings with, usually in order to express disapproval or to force acceptance of certain conditions.

CIVIL RIGHTS
A guarantee of equal social opportunities and equal protection under the law, regardless of gender, race, religion, or other personal traits.

CONVENTION
A gathering of like-minded people to discuss an issue or group of issues.

CORPORATION
A large business, often one with such power that it has widespread influence over a nation.

DECLARATION
A document that outlines the demands and positions of a person or group.

DISCRIMINATION
Unfair treatment of other people, usually because of race, age, or gender.

DISSENT
To express a different opinion from others.

DUTIES
Taxes paid on the import or export of goods.

EQUALITY
A situation in which people are all treated in the same fashion, without favoritism.

IMMORAL
Behavior that goes against accepted views of right and wrong.

INDICTED
To bring a formal charge against by a jury.

MARTYR
Someone who suffers or dies for a belief or principle.

PROTEST
To formally act against something, in opposition to it.

REPUBLICAN PARTY
One of the two major political parties in the United States. Generally considered more conservative.

SEGREGATION
The practice of separating groups of people based on race, gender, ethnicity, or other factors.

SUFFRAGE
The right to vote in a political election.

TEAR GAS
A nerve gas that acts against the body's pain sensors. People who are gassed cry, cough, and vomit.

UNION
A formal organization of workers.

ADDITIONAL RESOURCES

SELECTED BIBLIOGRAPHY

Boyle, Francis Anthony. *Protesting Power: War, Resistance, and Law.* Lanham, MD: Rowman & Littlefield, 2007. Print.

Daniel L. Schofield, S.J.D. "Controlling Public Protest: First Amendment Implications." *FBI Law Enforcement Bulletin* November 1994: 25–32. Print.

Michener, James. *Kent State: What Happened and Why.* New York: Random House, 1971. Print.

Roberts, Adam, and Timothy Garton Ash. *Civil Resistance and Power Politics: The Experience of Non-Violent Action from Gandhi to the Present.* Oxford, UK: Oxford UP, 2009. Print.

FURTHER READINGS

Capek, Michael. *Civil Rights Movement.* Minneapolis, MN: Abdo, 2014. Print.

Greenwald, Dara, and Josh MacPhee, eds. *Signs of Change: Social Movement Cultures, 1960s to Now.* Oakland, CA: AK Press, 2010. Print.

Lusted, Marcia Amidon. *Tinker v. Des Moines: The Right to Protest in Schools.* Minneapolis, MN: Abdo, 2013. Print.

Yellin, Eric S. *Racism in the Nation's Service: Government Workers and the Color Line in Woodrow Wilson's America.* Chapel Hill, NC: U of North Carolina P, 2016. Print.

ONLINE RESOURCES

To learn more about the right to protest, visit **abdobooklinks.com**. These links are routinely monitored and updated to provide the most current information available.

MORE INFORMATION

For more information on this subject, contact or visit the following organizations:

AMERICAN CIVIL LIBERTIES UNION

125 Broad Street
New York, NY 10004
212-549-2500

aclu.org

This organization aims to protect the individual rights and liberties of all Americans guaranteed by the Constitution of the United States.

SUPREME COURT OF THE UNITED STATES

1 First Street NE
Washington, DC 20543
202-479-3000

supremecourt.gov

The Supreme Court of the United States is the highest federal court in the country and hands down the final decision on many issues.

SOURCE NOTES

CHAPTER 1. GUNNED DOWN

1. Jerry M. Lewis and Thomas R. Hensley. "The May 4 Shootings at Kent State University: The Search for Historical Accuracy." *Kent State University*. Kent State University, n.d. Web. 7 Sept. 2017.

2. Thomas M. Grace. *Kent State: Death and Dissent in the Long Sixties*. Amherst, MA: U of Massachusetts P, 2016. Print. 3-4.

3. "'My God! They're Killing Us': Newsweek's 1970 Coverage of the Kent State Shooting." *Newsweek*. Newsweek LLC, 4 May 2015. Web. 7 Sept. 2017.

4. "1970 Year in Review: Kent State Shootings." *UPI*. United Press International, Inc., 1970. Web. 7 Sept. 2017.

5. "Kent State Shooting Divided Campus and Country." *NPR*. NPR, 3 May 2010. Web. 7 Sept. 2017.

6. Yevgeny Yevtushenko. "Flowers and Bullets." *Kent State University*. Kent State University, n.d. Web. 7 Sept. 2017.

CHAPTER 2. A LONG HISTORY

1. "Jamestown Colony." *History*. A&E Television Networks, 2010. Web. 7 Sept. 2017.

2. Frank E. Grizzard and D. Boyd Smith. *Jamestown Colony: A Political, Social, and Cultural History*. Santa Barbara, CA: ABC-CLIO, 2007. Print. 171.

3. Ibid.

4. "Boston Tea Party." *Britannica*. Encyclopedia Britannica Inc., n.d. Web. 26 Sept. 2017.

CHAPTER 3. TURMOIL IN THE 1800S

1. "Slavery in America." *History*. A&E Television Networks, 2009. Web. 7 Sept. 2017.

2. Christopher Hamner. "The Disaster of an Innovation." *Teaching History*. Roy Rosenzweig Center for History and New Media at George Mason University, n.d. Web. 7 Sept. 2017.

3. "Nat Turner." *History*. A&E Television Networks, 2009. Web. 7 Sept. 2017.

4. Jennifer Greiman and Paul Stasi. *The Last Western: Deadwood and the End of American Empire*. New York: Bloomsbury Publishing, 2012. Print. 28.

5. "The Great Railroad Strike of 1877." *Martinsburg Roundhouse*. Martinsburg Roundhouse, n.d. Web. 7 Sept. 2017.

6. Bernhard C. Korn. "Labor Seeks Its Own." *The Story of Bay View*. Milwaukee, WI: Milwaukee County Historical Society, 1980. Print. 85–89.

CHAPTER 4. WOMEN'S SUFFRAGE

1. "Sojourner Truth." *Biography*. A&E Television Networks, 27 Apr. 2017. Web. 7 Sept. 2017.

2. Lori D. Ginzberg. *Elizabeth Cady Stanton: An American Life*. New York: Hill and Wang, 2010. Print. 127.

3. Bernadette D. Proctor, Jessica L. Semega, and Melissa A. Kollar. "Income and Poverty in the United States: 2015." *United States Census Bureau*. US Department of Commerce, 20 Apr. 2017. Web. 7 Sept. 2017.

4. Eileen Patten. "Racial, Gender Wage Gaps Persist in U.S. Despite Some Progress." *Pew Research Center*. Pew Research Center, 1 July 2016. Web. 7 Sept. 2017.

5. Jessica Ravitz. "The New Women Warriors: Reviving the Fight for Equal Rights." *CNN*. Turner Broadcasting System, Inc., 16 Apr. 2015. Web. 7 Sept. 2017.

6. Kenneth K. Walsh. "The 1960s: A Decade of Change for Women." *U.S. News & World Report*. U.S. News & World Report LP, 12 Mar. 2010. Web. 7 Sept. 2017.

SOURCE NOTES CONTINUED

CHAPTER 5. THE CIVIL RIGHTS MOVEMENT

1. "16 Martin Luther King Quotes to Remember." *Amnesty International.* Amnesty International, 15 Jan. 2016. Web. 7 Sept. 2017.

2. "Montgomery Bus Boycott." *History.* A&E Television Networks, 2010. Web. 7 Sept. 2017.

3. "The Greensboro Chronology." *International Civil Rights Center and Museum.* International Civil Rights Center and Museum, n.d. Web. 7 Sept. 2017.

4. Jan Blakeslee. "'White Flight' to the Suburbs: A Demographic Approach." *Institute for Research on Poverty.* Institute for Research on Poverty, 1979. Web. 7 Sept. 2017.

CHAPTER 6. WAR PROTESTS

1. Eric A. Gordon. "Today in History: 50th Anniversary of the First National March Against Vietnam War." *People's World.* People's World, 17 Apr. 2015. Web. 7 Sept. 2017.

2. "The Pacifica Radio/UC Berkeley Social Activism Sound Recording Project: Anti-Vietnam War Protests in the San Francisco Bay Area and Beyond." *University of California, Berkeley Library.* University of California, Berkeley, n.d. Web. 7 Sept. 2017.

3. "Johnson Says U.S. Should Stay in Vietnam." *History.* A&E Television Networks, 2009. Web. 7 Sept. 2017.

4. "Tinker v. Des Moines Independent Community School District." *Justia US Supreme Court.* Justia, n.d. Web. 7 Sept. 2017.

5. Arthur G. Neal. *National Trauma and Collective Memory: Extraordinary Events in the American Experience.* Abingdon, UK: Routledge, 2005. Print. 93.

6. "My Lai Massacre." *History.* A&E Television Networks, 2009. Web. 7 Sept. 2017.

7. "Brief History of Chicago's 1968 Democratic Convention." *All Politics CNN Time.* All Politics, 1997. Web. 7 Sept. 2017.

8. "This Day in History: U.S. Withdraws from Vietnam." *History.* A&E Television Networks, 2009. Web. 7 Sept. 2017.

CHAPTER 7. PROTESTING IN THE DIGITAL AGE

1. "2011: Occupy Wall Street." *National Geographic*. National Geographic Society, n.d. Web. 7 Sept. 2017.

2. Adam Martin. "How Occupy Wall Street Spent $700,000 in Six Months." *The Atlantic*. The Atlantic Monthly Group, 13 Mar. 2012. Web. 7 Sept. 2017.

3. "November 17: Historic Day of Action for the 99%." *Occupy Wall Street*. Occupy Solidarity Network, 18 Nov. 2011. Web. 7 Sept. 2017.

4. Erin Baldassari. "Oakland: Election Protesters Lead Police on 5-mile March." *East Bay Times*. Digital First Media, 26 Nov. 2016. Web. 7 Sept. 2017.

CHAPTER 8. THE RESULTS

1. Dan Kopf. "A Harvard Study Identified the Precise Reason Protests Are an Effective Way to Cause Political Change." *Quartz*. Quartz, 3 Feb. 2017. Web. 7 Sept. 2017.

2. "Trayvon Martin Shooting Fast Facts." *CNN*. Turner Broadcasting System, Inc., 22 June 2017. Web. 7 Sept. 2017.

3. "Statement by the President." *The White House: President Barack Obama*. USA.gov, 14 Aug. 2014. Web. 7 Sept. 2017.

INDEX

ABOUT THE AUTHOR

DUCHESS HARRIS, JD, PHD

Professor Harris is the chair of the American Studies Department at Macalester College. The author and coauthor of four books (*Hidden Human Computers: The Black Women of NASA* and *Black Lives Matter* with Sue Bradford Edwards, *Racially Writing the Republic: Racists, Race Rebels, and Transformations of American Identity* with Bruce Baum, and *Black Feminist Politics from Kennedy to Clinton/Obama*), she has been an associate editor for *Litigation News*, the American Bar Association Section's quarterly flagship publication, and was the first editor-in-chief of *Law Raza Journal*, an interactive online race and the law journal for William Mitchell College of Law.

She has earned a PhD in American Studies from the University of Minnesota and a Juris Doctorate from William Mitchell College of Law.

10/18